HURRY, MURRY!

TEXT **Tan Yi Lin**
ILLUSTRATIONS **Nanimonda**

mc **Marshall Cavendish**
Children

Text © 2023 Tan Yi Lin
Illustrations © 2023 Nanimonda
Editor: Melanie Lee

Published by Marshall Cavendish Children
An imprint of Marshall Cavendish International

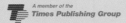

A member of the
Times Publishing Group

Other Marshall Cavendish Offices:
Marshall Cavendish Corporation, 800 Westchester Ave, Suite N-641, Rye Brook, NY 10573, USA • Marshall Cavendish International (Thailand) Co Ltd, 253 Asoke, 16th Floor, Sukhumvit 21 Road, Klongtoey Nua, Wattana, Bangkok 10110, Thailand • Marshall Cavendish (Malaysia) Sdn Bhd, Times Subang, Lot 46, Subang Hi-Tech Industrial Park, Batu Tiga, 40000 Shah Alam, Selangor Darul Ehsan, Malaysia

Marshall Cavendish is a registered trademark of Times Publishing Limited

National Library Board, Singapore Cataloguing-in-Publication Data

Name(s): Tan, Yi Lin. | Nanimonda, illustrator.
Title: Hurry Murry! / text, Tan Yi Lin ; illustrations, Nanimonda.
Description: Singapore : Marshall Cavendish Children, [2023]
Identifier(s): ISBN 978-981-5044-36-2 (paperback)
Subject(s): LCSH: Sloths--Juvenile fiction. | Success--Juvenile fiction.
Classification: DDC 428.6--dc23

Printed in Singapore

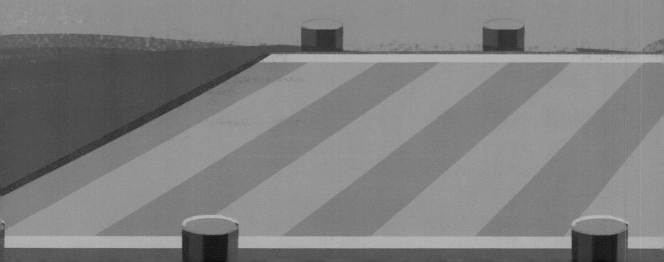

To Colette, Claire and Candace
whom I have hurried many times over:
Be not hurried by the world.
Make success at your own pace.

Murry was a sloth.

He liked to hang from trees,
eat vegetables, and sleep a lot.

He was also slow.

Others were always hurrying Murry.

"Hurry, Murry!"
his teacher said.

"Hurry, Murry!"
his friends shouted.

"Hurry, Murry,"
the lunch lady coaxed.

"But I'm still chewing on my
breakfast," replied Murry.

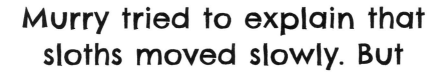

Murry tried to explain that
sloths moved slowly. But

"Hurry, Murry!"

was all everyone said to him.
All the time.

Murry tried using his imagination to make himself move faster.

Nothing worked.
He just could not be rushed.

"I wish everyone could see
that I'm doing my best,"
he said with a sigh.

Only his family understood.
They never hurried Murry.

Murry also had a secret wish.
He dreamt of being good
at sports.

But "Hurry, Murry!" was all his friends and coach told him during physical education lessons.

One day, Murry's class
set off on a trip to the shore.
They were learning to wakeboard!

Everyone was excited!

"I will be the fastest!" boasted Cheetah.

"Not as fast as I!" hooted Monkey.

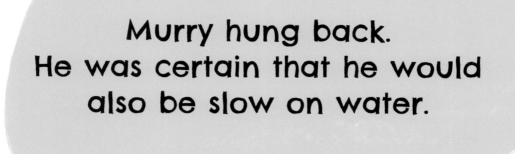

Murry hung back.
He was certain that he would
also be slow on water.

"Stand up slowly on the board,"
said Panda, their teacher.

"Don't hurry."

Cheetah went first. He took one swift leap and splashed into the water.

"Don't hurry," said Panda.

Monkey went next.
He jumped up quickly
and fell on his bottom.

"Don't hurry,"
said Panda.

It was Murry's turn.
He held the rope and waited.

The boat started moving.
Murry waited.

The boat moved faster.
Murry waited.

The boat moved even faster.
Still, Murry waited.

Ever so slowly,
Murry pushed
up onto his legs.

Ever so slowly, he
moved one foot in
front of the other.

Ever so slowly,
he stood up on
the board.

Murry was wakeboarding!

"Hurray, Murry!" cheered his friends.

With each slow and steady action, Murry moved the board across the water.

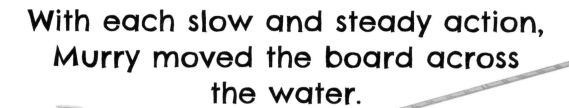

Up and down.

Side to side.

Very fast. Just like how he had always dreamt of moving.

"Hurray, Murry! Hurray, Murry!" cheered everyone.

When Murry got home, he told his family about how he was the fastest in wakeboarding in his class.

"How did you do it, Murry?"
they asked.

"I didn't hurry," said Murry proudly.
"Not a single bit."

About the Author

Growing up in Singapore, **Tan Yi Lin** spent weekends at
second-hand bookstores browsing through tales of talking
animals, globetrotting adventures, and travels to whimsical
lands. She still does the same with her 3 daughters.
Outside of her job in the public service, Yi Lin writes
stories inspired by childhood and a blog for an adopted
Doxiepoo named Miso.

About the Illustrator

Nanimonda is an illustrator who loves animals and stories.
She believes that stories can be told in any medium
and has experimented with them in various ways. These
range from making art installations, to drawing game art.
However, her favourite way of storytelling is through
looping animated illustrations.encountered digital art.
Since then, digital painting has been her passion
and medium of choice.